Don't miss these other books
based on Scooby-Doo 2:
Monsters Unleashed

Scooby-Doo 2 Movie Novelization
Scooby-Doo 2 Monster Joke Book
Scooby-Doo 2 Movie Storybook
Scooby-Doo 2 Movie Reader

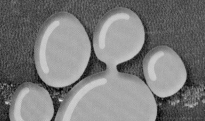

SCOOBY DOO 2
MONSTERS UNLEASHED
BOOK OF MONSTERS

by Howie Dewin

THE OFFICIAL MOVIE SCRAPBOOK

Scholastic Inc.

New York   Toronto   London   Auckland   Sydney
Mexico City   New Delhi   Hong Kong   Buenos Aires

ISBN 0-439-56756-4

Designed by Louise Bova

12 11 10 9 8 7 6 5 4 3   4 5 6 7 8 9/0

Printed in the U.S.A.

First printing, March 2004

MONSTER HALL OF FAME

Check out our -EST Gallery ... the dumbEST, meanEST, smartEST monsters Mystery, Inc. has ever known!

REDBEARD'S GHOST
"Most Hair-Raising"

GIGGLING GREEN GHOST
"Brightest (and Greenest)"

THE GHOST CLOWN

"Best Entertainer"

CHICKENSTEIN

"Fowl-est"

MINER 49ER

"Most Picky"

NAME: THE EVIL MASKED FIGURE

APPEARANCE: Evil and masked

SPECIAL SKILLS: Scaring the daylights out of Scooby and Shaggy.

EVIL DEEDS: Laughing insanely. Making real monsters out of fake ones.

HISTORY: Who knows? We don't know who he really is . . . or at least, not yet!

PETS: Pterodactyl Ghost

SCRAPPED? That remains to be seen!

"This time, Mystery, Inc., you'll be the ones who are unmasked — as the buffons you truly are!"

" . . . soon Coolsville will be mine!"

How Do You Know When You've Met a Monster? BY DAPHNE

When searching for monsters, it's super important to know exactly what you're looking for. Here are a few things to look for when you're out capturing your own villains. You know you've met a monster when you observe . . .

. . . a curious bright green skin tone.

... a large fish tank where a head should be.

... a noticeable lack of skin.

NAME: CREEPER

APPEARANCE: Dead on his feet.

HOBBIES: Touring cemeteries, drag racing with 18-wheeler trucks.

EVIL DEED: Projectile vomiting on innocent citizens.

SCRAPPED? Dead. Again.

"Jeepers! It's the Creeper!"

"Monsters are trying to kill us!"

"Excuse me, sir, do you have anything to say for yourself?"

PICTURE PERFECT:
Fred's Greatest Moments

NAME: FRED JONES

JOB: Leader of Mystery, Inc.

APPEARANCE: Blond hair and dark eyes

FAVORITE PHRASES: "I guess that wraps up another mystery!"; "Let's split up and look for clues."

LIKES: Inventing gadgets; solving mysteries; being strong and manly; Daphne

DISLIKES: Getting tricked by villains

"Hey, girls! I brought an ascot for each of you."

"They've found us!"

"Baby, you're still the most beautiful girl in Coolsville to me . . ."

". . . a good detective must always give the impression that he's in control."

"Of course lil' old Coolsville can solve its problems without us . . ."

"Bring it!"

NAME: BLACK KNIGHT GHOST

APPEARANCE: Big and black. Carries a ridiculously dangerous sword.

NICKNAME: Metalhead

HOBBIES: Fencing and horseback riding

EVIL DEED: Acting as the Evil Masked Figure's right-hand monster.

HISTORY: He was created by Old Man Wickles.

SCRAPPED? Consider him scrap metal! He had, like, a total meltdown.

"You'll go nowhere, knave."

"Nighty-night, knight."

"Like, the Black Knight Ghost!"

"Talking is for wimps."

Fair and Balanced Reporter or Just an Old-Fashioned Menace?

NAME: HEATHER JASPER HOWE

APPEARANCE: Awfully pretty

HEIGHT: Just right

WEIGHT: Perfect

EVIL DEEDS: Flirting with Fred. Misquoting Fred. Upsetting Fred. Insulting Daphne.

SCRAPPED? Don't know if she needs to be scrapped . . .

NAME: NED

APPEARANCE: A blur

EVIL DEEDS: Hyper camera work. Helping Heather ruin Mystery, Inc.'s reputation.

SCRAPPED? Not yet . . .

"Thanks a lot! The scoop of the night, gone!
Can't you do anything right?"

"I beg you, Mystery, Inc. If you can hear me, turn yourselves in!"

NAME: PTERODACTYL GHOST

NICKNAME: Birdbrain, Tweety

APPEARANCE: Unattractive prehistoric flying reptile

HEIGHT: As high as it can fly

WEIGHT: Light as a bird

EVIL DEED: Responsible for a statewide crime spree.

SCRAPPED? Like, totally grounded!

"Aaaaahhhh!"

NAME: SKELETON MEN

APPEARANCE: One eyeball each . . . that's pretty much all you need to know

NICKNAME: Ocular Ogre

SPECIAL SKILL: 20-Nothing Vision

HEIGHT: Tall enough to be scary

WEIGHT: Bone-thin

HOBBIES: Making annoying squeaky noises. Taking each other apart and building things with their bones. Eyeball shooting.

EVIL DEED: Being ultra-ungroovy and picking on Shaggy and Scooby.

SCRAPPED? Like any good dog with a bone, Scooby buried them!

IMAGE IS EVERYTHING:
Daphne's Greatest Moments

NAME: DAPHNE BLAKE

JOB: Being a beautiful teenager

APPEARANCE: Red hair and dark eyes

FAVORITE PHRASES: "Jeepers"; "I don't see anything to be afraid of."

LIKES: A good mystery; keeping up her appearance; Fred

DISLIKES: Getting kidnapped by villains

"Daphne! We love you!"

"Scooby, those *so* don't go with that sweater."

"I enjoy being a girl."

"Taste the pain, Mr. Glowy-Ugly-Thing."

"It's never too late to learn to properly apply makeup!"

Turn the page for your own ultra-groovy poster from the Scooby-Doo movie.

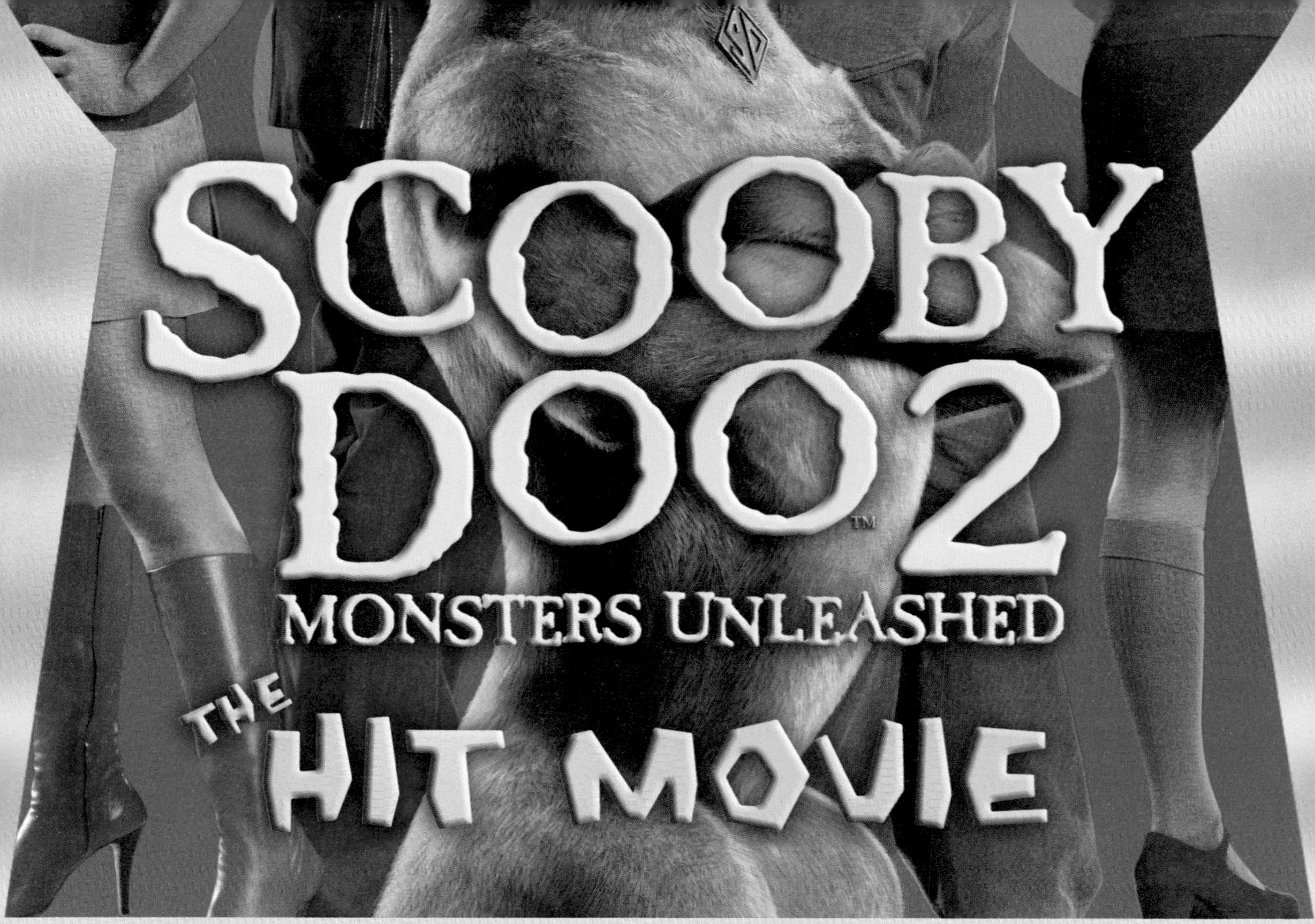
SCOOBY DOO2™
MONSTERS UNLEASHED
THE HIT MOVIE

NAME: MINER 49ER

APPEARANCE: Giant bearded man

HOBBIES: Pickax tossing. Breathing fire.

EVIL DEED: Doesn't mine his manners when he picks his victims.

SCRAPPED? Gassed! (Your gas is as good as mine.)

"You're mine! Get it? MINE!"

"We can make this easy or hard. Take. Your. Pick!"

"The Miner 49er!"

EVIL CAN BE TOUGH TO SPOT: Is He or Isn't He?

NAME: JEREMIAH WICKLES

NICKNAME: Old Man Wickles

APPEARANCE: Eerie, ugly senior citizen

HOBBIES: Supernatural stuff

EVIL DEED: Also known as the Black Knight Ghost

HISTORY: He was Jonathan Jacobo's cellmate in prison and was recently released.

SCRAPPED? Remains to be seen. . . .

"I'll call the cops on you, you diabolic boppers!"

"Have you done anything, like, really cool and evil lately?"

"I don't know nothing about no monsters!"

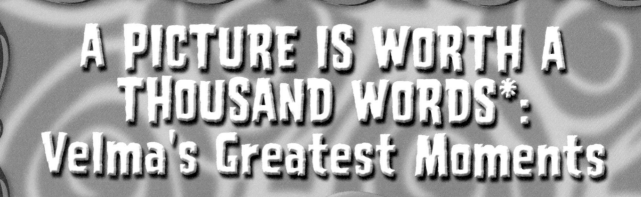

A PICTURE IS WORTH A THOUSAND WORDS*: Velma's Greatest Moments

NAME: VELMA DINKLEY

JOB: Being a super-smart teenager

APPEARANCE: Dark brown hair and dark eyes

FAVORITE PHRASES: "Jinkies!"; "I think we've got our mystery solved."

LIKES: A good puzzle; reviewing the facts of a mystery after it's been solved; science; museum curator Patrick Wisely

DISLIKES: Not recognizing the importance of a clue immediately

*or roughly 6,748 letters, considering the average number of letters per word in the English Dictionary.

"Like . . . a . . . a . . . date?"

"I only trust facts! They don't let you down!"

"...a glamorous and mysterious jet-set adventurer who's preoccupied with international intrigue and all.... Yeah, that's me."

"Jinkies!"

"...a most wonderful clue.... This is a real pterodactyl scale! I'm still probing its chemical composition."

EVIL MASTERMIND

"See you later, suckers!"

NAME: JONATHAN JACOBO

APPEARANCE: Sunken face, pure white hair

HEIGHT: Flexible, depending on disguise

WEIGHT: Same as above

HOBBIES: Anything supernatural

EVIL DEED: He tried to create a monster army.

HOW BAD IS HE? He stole Jeremiah Wickles' tater tots when they were in prison.

HISTORY: He was the original Pterodactyl Ghost and masterminded a statewide crime spree. After the gang captured him, he went to prison. Three years ago, he tried to escape by recreating his Pterodactyl Flying Machine. He crashed into the ocean and his body was never found.

SCRAPPED? Unmasked! Again and again.

"Come alive! Alive!"

"...a shrine to Jonathan Jacobo?"

NAME: CHICKENSTEIN

APPEARANCE: Moist and meaty

HEIGHT: Tall for a chicken

WEIGHT: At $2.69 a pound, he's worth a fortune!

EVIL DEED: Terrified the gang and an entire newspaper staff.

HISTORY: Tried to destroy Fred's uncle's newspaper.

SCRAPPED? He'll never cross another road.

NAME: CLOWN GHOST

APPEARANCE: Funny hair. Curiously round, red nose.

HOBBY: Hypnotizing innocent teenage detectives.

EVIL DEED: Tried to ruin the circus by convincing the troupe it was jinxed!

HISTORY: Went to prison for stealing.

SCRAPPED? We made him a laughingstock!

NAME: NORVILLE "SHAGGY" ROGERS

JOB: Teenager

APPEARANCE: Brown hair and black eyes

FAVORITE PHRASE: "Zoinks!"

LIKES: Food — lots of it; his best pal, Scooby-Doo

DISLIKES: Ghosts, monsters, and scary stuff in general

"We're . . . screw-ups. We have to be more like real detectives. You know, use our intelligent-ive-ness-icity."

"Detectives do go undercover, don't they?"

"Ah — clues. Alas!"

"Cluetopia!"

"A UFO — an unidentified freaky object!"

"What up, bro?"

NAME: CAPTAIN CUTLER'S GHOST

APPEARANCE: Salty old devil covered in seaweed

HOBBIES: Scuba diving in heavy metal. Spear gun target practice. Water sports.

EVIL DEED: Sailing his ghost ship down public streets.

HISTORY: Boat hijacker who interrupted Scooby while he was surfing.

SCRAPPED? Sunk!

"Zoinks! Captain Cutler's Ghost!"

"Like, color me hyperventilating, man!"

"Nooooooo!"

HOW WE SOLVE CRIMES

by Velma

Thanks to our success as teenage detectives, Mystery, Inc. are heroes to all of Coolsville. But remember, we've been fighting crime and unmasking villains for a long time. Fred, Daphne, Scooby, Shaggy, and I have developed our skills and worked hard to improve our natural talents. How do we solve crimes and defeat our foes? Take a look.

We never neglect the basic tools of the trade.

We don't underestimate the importance of appearance.

We never let them see us sweat.

We always remember the importance of exercise.

We never forget the importance of a good book.

How do we know when we've defeated the villain? We hear them say: "And I would have gotten away with it, too, if it weren't for you meddling punks and your dumb dog!"

Dreamboat or Evil Mastermind: Is He or Isn't He? Part II

NAME: PATRICK WISELY

APPEARANCE: Really cute

HEIGHT: Exactly right for Velma

WEIGHT: Just perfect for Velma

EVIL DEED: He completely freaked out three-fifths of the gang. Although what freaked out Shaggy and Scooby was MUCH different from what freaked out Velma!

SCRAPPED? Velma hopes not. . . .

"You're just so easy to scare!"

"This time I'd like to go out with you as myself."

"Do you have to go to the bathroom?"

"My museum!"

DOGGONE PHOTOGENIC!
Scooby's Greatest Moments

NAME: SCOOBERT "SCOOBY" DOO

JOB: Man's Best Friend (Daphne and Velma's too)

APPEARANCE: Brown with black spots

HEIGHT: 12 paws high

FAVORITE PHRASES: "Scooby-Dooby-Doo!"; "Relp!"

LIKES: Scooby Snacks, pizza, ice cream, and all other kinds of food; his best pal, Shaggy

DISLIKES: Things that go bump in the night

"Ri'm ready!"

"Rikes!"

"Shake it!"

"Rhat ronster?"

A PICTURE QUIZ
by Shaggy and Scooby

Now that Scooby and I have decided to become brainiac detectives like the rest of the gang, I've made a few very intelligent observations. It's always good to keep your eye on the little things. Detecting is in the details.

Rid rou ray, "da tail"?

Use your powers of observation. Which member of the gang is fighting which monster?

1.
_____ vs. _____

2.
_____ vs. _____

3.
_____ vs. _____

4.
_____ vs. _____

1. Shaggy vs. the Black Knight Ghost; 2. Fred vs. the Black Knight Ghost; 3. Scooby vs. the Skeleton Men; 4. Shaggy vs. Miner 49er